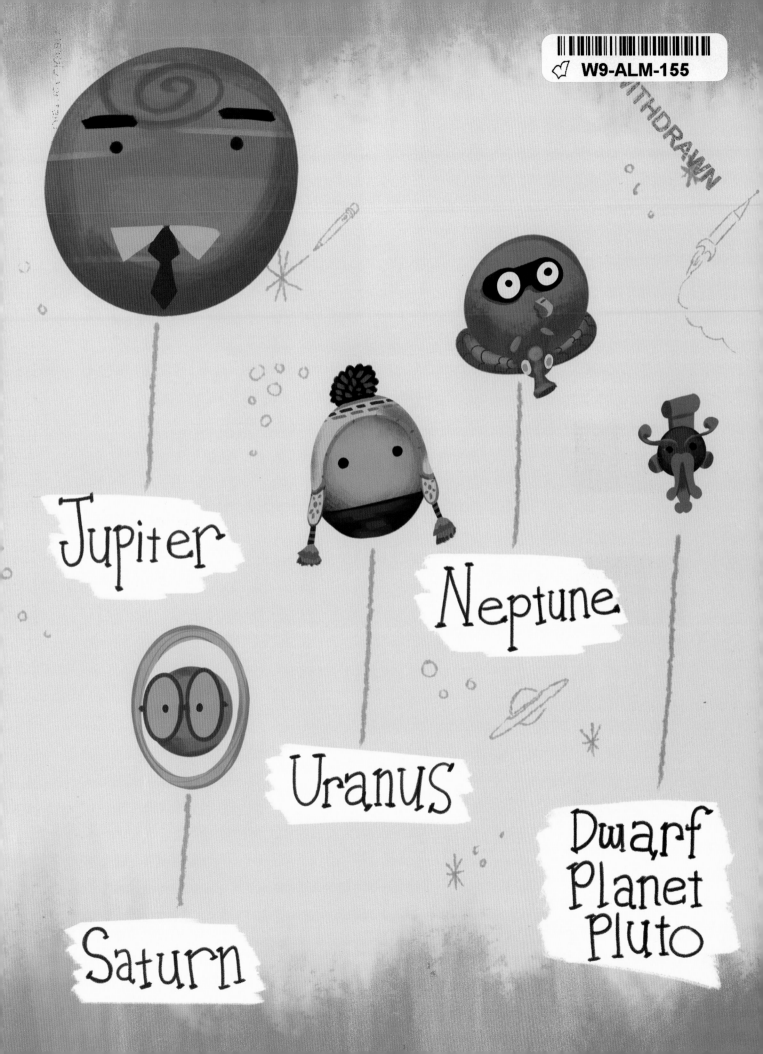

Jupiter

Neptune

Uranus

Dwarf Planet Pluto

Saturn

For Dad

Special thank you to Dr. Chris McCarthy
at San Francisco State University
—DU

For Megan and Kai, my sun and moon
—JL

About This Book

The illustrations for this book were hand-illustrated digitally using Adobe Photoshop. This book was edited by Esther Cajahuaringa and designed by Lynn El-Roeiy with art direction from Saho Fujii. The production was supervised by Lillian Sun and Kimberly Stella, and the production editor was Annie McDonnell. The text was set in Chauncy Decaf Medium and Fontoon ITC.

XO, EXOPLANET

By Deborah Underwood

Illustrated by Jorge Lacera

L B
Little, Brown and Company
New York Boston

The planets were swirling around the sun, as usual, when Neptune discovered something.

"What do you see?"
asked dwarf planet Pluto.

"I see a planet! But it's not circling our sun.
It's circling another star, far, far away!"

Jupiter called a meeting.
"We will send a letter of greeting," he said.

"What should we say?" asked Mercury.
"And what should we call the planet?"

"This planet is OUTSIDE our solar system.
Exo means 'outside.' So we will call it
an exoplanet," said Venus.

Jupiter dictated:

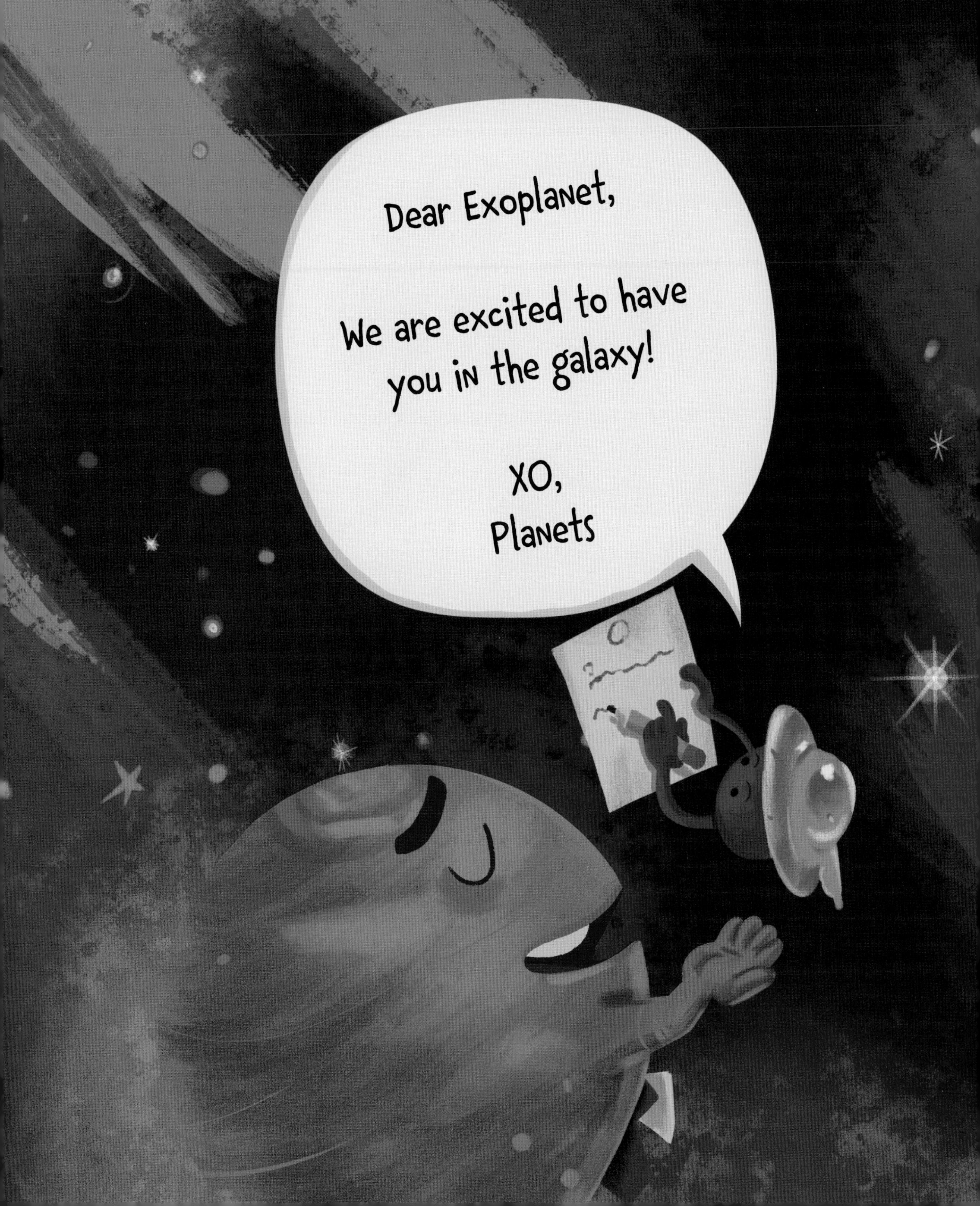

It took a while for the planets to hear back.
(Fortunately, planets have lots of time.)

Planets of THE Solar System

Dear Exoplanet,

An exoplanet is a planet circling a star that is not the sun.

XO,
Planets

EXPRESS
SPACE
Dear Exoplanets,
I'm afraid you are mistaken.
I AM circling the sun.
MY sun.
YOU are the exoplanets.
XO,
Just Plain Planet

Planets of THE solar system
Dear EXOPLANET,
We are looking around our SUN.
We don't see you. So YOU are the EXOPLANET.
XO,
Planets
Dear EXOPLANETS,
I am looking around MY SUN. I don't see you. So YOU are the exoplanets.
Period.
Period.
Period.
No erasies.
XO,
Planet

"Mercury, write this!"

DEAR EXOPLANET,

YOU ARE THE EXOPLANET!
YOU ARE OUT OF OUR SOLAR SYSTEM!
JUST LIKE WE ARE OUT OF PATIENCE!
DO NOT BOTHER TO WRITE BACK!

XO,
P-L-A-N-E-T-S

The planets orbited the sun in silence.
And space was a little more lonely.

After a while, a comet flew by, as she did from time to time.
"What's wrong?" she asked.

We found an exoplanet, and she says WE'RE the exoplanets!
Exoplanet, SCHMECKSOPLANET! We're planets!
I am FAR too important to be an exoplanet!

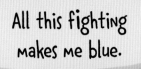

All this fighting makes me blue.

It's scary when Jupiter gets mad.

It's hard for us rings to be around Saturn when they're sulking.

What if we really are exoplanets?

I miss the exoplanet.

Me too.

Everyone, please calm down. Mercury, is Earth big or small?
Big! Earth is more than twice my size!

Jupiter, is Earth big or small?
Small! You could fit more than 1,000 Earths inside me!

Uranus, is Mars hot or cold?
Hot! Look how close he is to the sun!
Solar System
Mercury
Venus
Earth
Mars
Jupiter
Saturn
Uranus
Neptune
Dwarf Planets

Venus, is Mars hot or cold?
Downright chilly. Look at his ice cap!

"I think we owe someone an apology," said Jupiter. "Mercury, please write this."

Dear Planet,

We are sorry. We understand now. To us, you are an exoplanet. But to you, *WE* are the exoplanets.

But no matter what anyone calls us, we are all round objects that travel around a star.

And we hope we can be friends.

XOXOXO,
(Your) Exoplanets

The exoplanet wrote back.

And space was a little less lonely again.

Dear Reader,

There really are exoplanets circling stars other than our sun. The first exoplanet orbiting a sunlike star was discovered in 1995. Now we've found thousands, with more being discovered each year.

Some exoplanets can be directly detected with powerful telescopes. Astronomers can also find exoplanets by observing stars. If a star's light gets dimmer, then bright again, it could be because an exoplanet passed in front of the star, blocking some of the star's light. And if a star wobbles a bit, it might be because an exoplanet is pulling on it as it circles the star.

Is there life on exoplanets? We don't know yet. I'm writing this letter in 2020, and the closest exoplanet we know of right now is so far away that it would take light more than four years to reach it—and light travels at 186,000 miles per second!

Astronomers are looking for ways to find life on these far-off planets without traveling to them. So in the future, maybe someone will make the exciting first discovery of exoplanet life.

Maybe that someone will be you.

XO,
The Author

P.S. When I was a kid, Pluto was a planet. Then the way scientists define "planet" changed, and Pluto became a dwarf planet instead. There are at least five dwarf planets—too many to put in this book, but I included Pluto as a tribute to the nine-planet solar system of my childhood.